For Christopher F.

First published in Great Britain in 1996 by Andersen Press Ltd., 20 Vauxhall Bridge Road, London SW1V
2SA. Published in Australia by Random House Australia Pty., 20 Alfred Street, Milsons Point, Sydney,
NSW 2061. All rights reserved. Colour separated in Switzerland by Photolitho AG, Zürich. Printed and
bound in Italy by Grafiche AZ, Verona.

10   9   8   7   6   5   4   3   2   1

British Library Cataloguing in Publication Data available.
ISBN 0 86264 702 9
This book has been printed on acid-free paper

THE TALE OF THE MONSTROUS TOAD

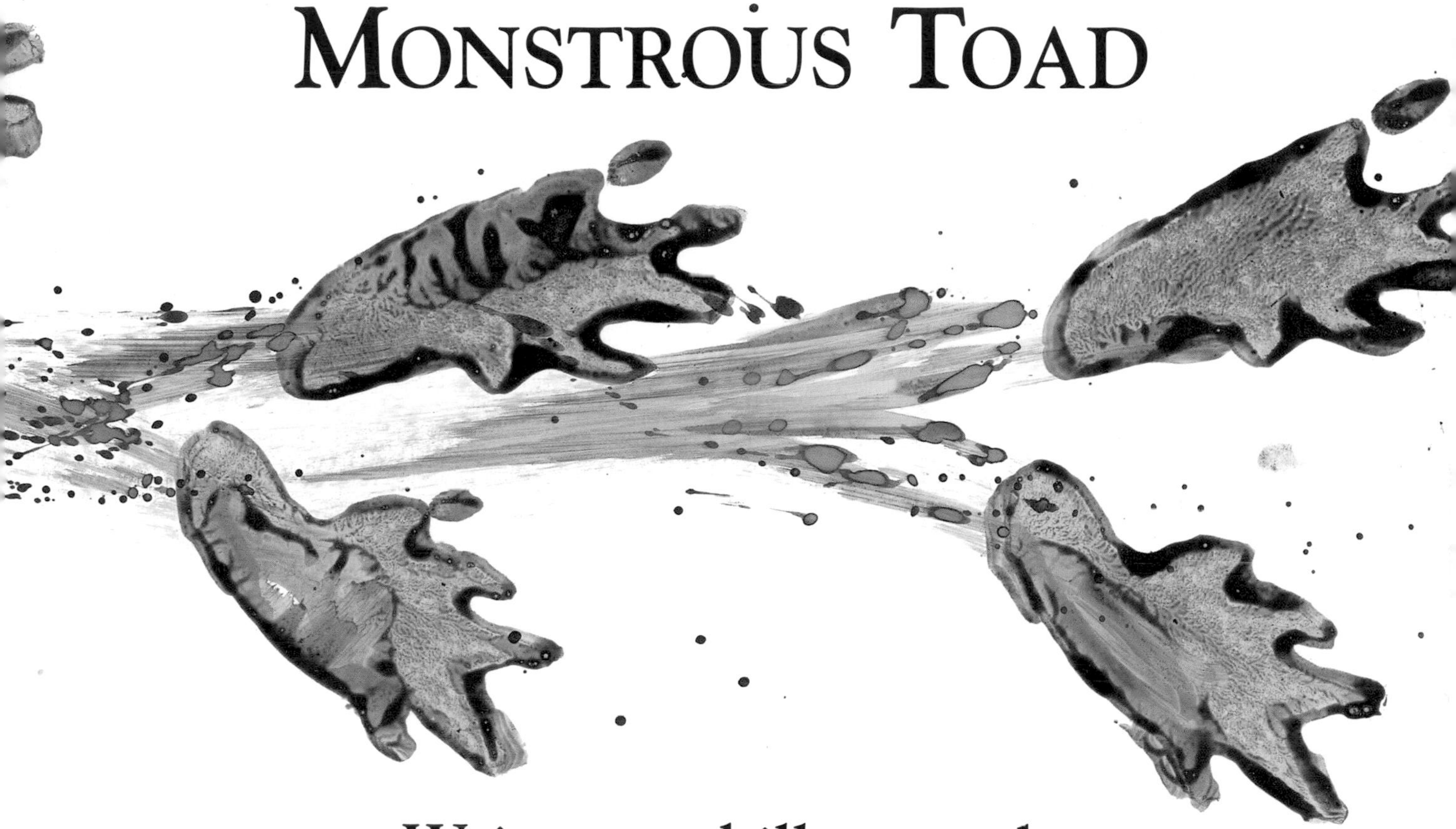

Written and illustrated
by Ruth Brown

Ⓐ

Andersen Press • London

42 T3

This is the tale of a monstrous toad,

a muddy toad, a slimy toad,
a clammy, sticky, gooey toad,

odorous, stinking, filthy and foul,
and smelling of stagnant water.

He's covered in warts and lumps and bumps,
stained and soiled, spotted and speckled,

poisonous, septic, toxic and bitter,
and oozing venomous fluids.

The monstrous toad is a greedy toad, a
fly-munching, bug-crunching, worm-slurping toad.

He is clumsy, careless, short-sighted and slow,

and he waddles and stumbles,
winking and blinking,

straight into the jaws of a monster!

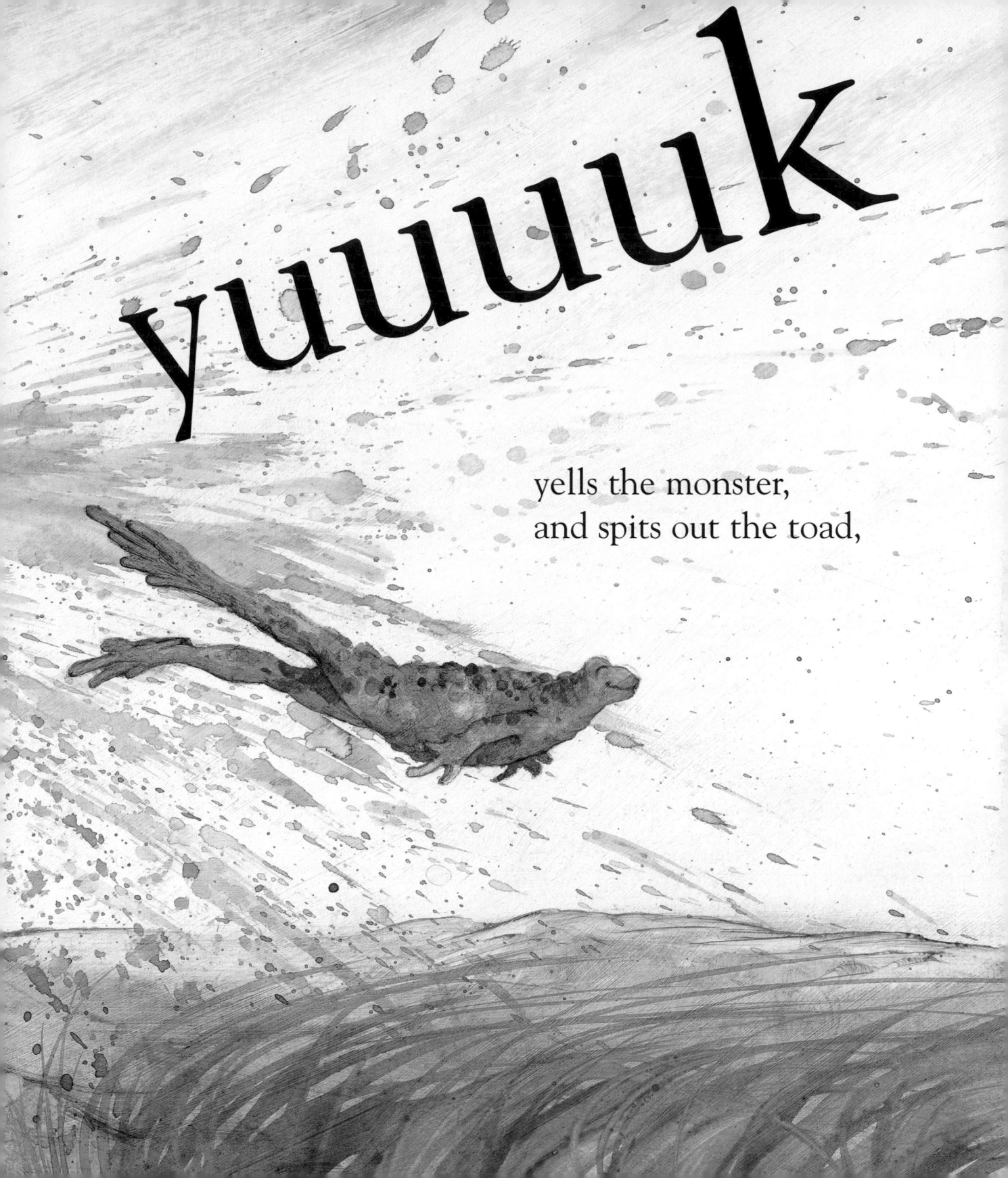

yuuuuk

yells the monster,
and spits out the toad,

the happy toad, the carefree toad,
the safe, secure, self-confident toad,

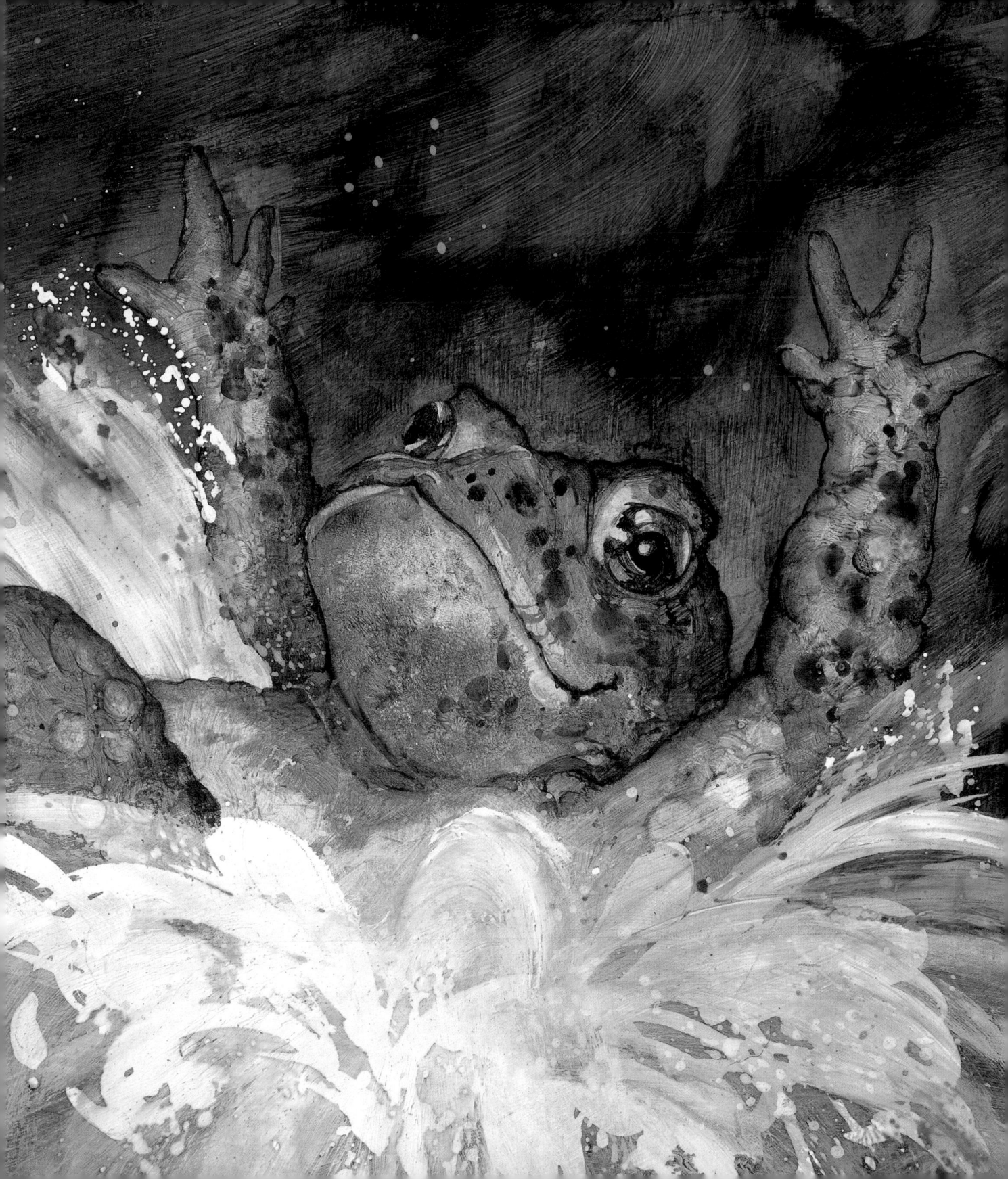

who smiles a monstrous smile.